THE FERGUSON LIBRARY

3 1 1 1 8 0 2 4 3 7 4 5 9 0

THE FERGUSON LIBRARY
WEED

P9-DOC-674

Cynthia Rylant • Arthur Howard

MOTOR MOUSE DELIVERS

THE FERGUSON LIBRARY
ONE PUBLIC LIBRARY PLAZA
STAMFORD, CONNECTICUT 06904

Beach Lane Books New York London Toronto Sydney New Delhi

BEACH LANE BOOKS
An imprint of Simon & Schuster Children's Publishing Division
1230 Avenue of the Americas, New York, New York 10020
Text copyright © 2020 by Cynthia Rylant
Illustrations copyright © 2020 by Arthur Howard
All rights reserved, including the right of reproduction in whole or in part in any form.
BEACH LANE BOOKS is a trademark of Simon & Schuster, Inc.
For information about special discounts for bulk purchases, please contact Simon & Schuster
Special Sales at 1-866-506-1949 or business@simonandschuster.com.
The Simon & Schuster Speakers Bureau can bring authors to your live event. For more
information or to book an event, contact the Simon & Schuster Speakers Bureau at
1-866-248-3049 or visit our website at www.simonspeakers.com.
Book design by Irene Metaxatos
The text for this book was set in Raleigh.
The illustrations for this book are rendered in mixed media.
Manufactured in China
0620 SCP
First Edition
10 9 8 7 6 5 4 3 2 1
Library of Congress Cataloging-in-Publication Data
Names: Rylant, Cynthia, author. | Howard, Arthur, illustrator.
Title: Motor Mouse delivers / Cynthia Rylant ; illustrated by Arthur Howard.
Description: First edition. | New York : Beach Lane Books, [2020] | Summary: Follows a busy
mouse as he plays an unusual game of croquet with his brother, makes deliveries by bus,
and reaches a crossroads.
Identifiers: LCCN 2019010141 | ISBN 9781481491280 (hardcover : alk. paper) |
ISBN 9781481491297 (eBook)
Subjects: | CYAC: Mice—Fiction.
Classification: LCC PZ7.R982 Mot 2020 | DDC [E]—dc23
LC record available at https://lccn.loc.gov/2019010141

CONTENTS

The Radio
Mystery Book

Motor Mouse loved a good story. He had always been quite the reader, and he always kept a tall stack of books beside his bed for nighttime reading.

At bedtime Motor Mouse enjoyed books that made him laugh or books that made him cry.

But he had a rule about one certain sort of book at bedtime, and that rule was this: NO!

"NO MYSTERIES!" declared Motor Mouse.

The reason for no mystery reading at bedtime is that mysteries always put Motor Mouse wide awake. Then when he wanted to go to sleep, he could not, and he found himself late in his kitchen buttering toast instead.

Motor Mouse had tried reading mystery books during the day, a snippet here and there, but he could never really sink his teeth into them. He was a bedtime reader.

Then one day his mystery life changed.

Motor Mouse was dialing his radio, searching for some band music, when one of the stations announced "The Radio Mystery Book."

"*What?*" said Motor Mouse. "Mysteries on the radio?"
Indeed.

It was a program that turned mystery books into shows on the radio.

Motor Mouse was mesmerized. He wished he'd made a cup of tea for listening, and he wanted to, but once the story started, there was no going anywhere near the kettle.

Every word will be vital, thought Motor Mouse.

So he sat straight in his chair and listened.

When Chapter One was finished, the program announced that Chapter Two would be tomorrow.

"*Tomorrow?*" cried Motor Mouse. He was not sure he could bear it, not knowing what happened next until tomorrow.

"If the hotel keeper opens that drawer," said Motor Mouse, "whatever will he find?"

He did not think he could wait another day to know. In fact, he was sure of it.

He drove his motorcar to the library.

Motor Mouse rushed inside and found the mystery book itself.

"Ah-HA!" said Motor Mouse. "Now I won't have to wait until tomorrow for Chapter Two."

He seated himself rather proudly at a table. He looked at the mystery book.

And at once, he did not want to open it.

"I am at a crossroads!" Motor Mouse called to a reader sitting at the other end of the long table.

"Shush!" the reader said, pointing to the QUIET sign.
"A crossroads!" cried Motor Mouse.

The reader moved to another table.

Motor Mouse groaned, all alone at his crossroads.

Should he open the book and read Chapter Two on his own *today?*

Or . . . should he wait and listen to the Radio Mystery Book with everyone else *tomorrow?*

Motor Mouse paused to remember how it felt to listen to the Radio Mystery Book. How his toes had tingled and his whiskers had wiggled.

Were there any tingling toes or wiggling whiskers happening now?

No.

Motor Mouse put the book back on its shelf and went home
to survive the day as best he could.

The *next* day, with a cup of tea well in hand, Motor Mouse sat down by the radio to listen to Chapter Two.

What the hotel keeper found in the drawer was the professor's *green glove.*

"Ha!" shouted Motor Mouse.

He could have found this out the day before at the library.

But Motor Mouse was happy he had waited. There can be great joy in anticipation.

And he reminded himself of this when he very nearly drove off to the library to read Chapter Three.

DAY OF THE DOUBLE-DECKER

All week Motor Mouse drove around town making deliveries. He was quite good at it, and his customers were always happy to see him.

On Mondays he delivered roses.
On Tuesdays he delivered oats.

On Wednesdays he delivered cloth.

And on Thursdays he delivered coffee beans.

The rest of the week was for lolling about, which he was also good at.

But one day the unthinkable happened. His motorcar would not start!

"*No!*" cried Motor Mouse in disbelief as he turned the key and heard nothing.

Motor Mouse rang his friend Winston, who was a mechanic. Winston came right over.

He looked at the motorcar from end to end. Then he shook his head.

"This car needs a week in the shop," Winston said, patting the car on its hood. "Happens to the best of them."

"But today is rose day," said Motor Mouse. "How will I make my delivery?"

"You can borrow my Bug if you like," said Winston.

But just then a double-decker bus rolled by.
The sign on it said, WE GO EVERYWHERE.
  "That's it!" said Motor Mouse. "I will take the bus!"

"The view from the upper deck is quite nice," said Winston.
"Yes!" said Motor Mouse.

The day was looking much better.
Winston promised to tow the car to his garage, and Motor Mouse ran to the bus shelter.

He found a route map and a timetable inside. Bus 74 would take him to the flower shop to pick up the roses. And Bus 15 would take him to the Sleepy Hen Inn where he always delivered them.

It would be an adventurous day!

When Bus 74 arrived, Motor Mouse bought a ticket from the driver and climbed the stairs to the upper deck.

Oh, lovely! thought Motor Mouse as he sat down and looked out over the town. He was practically at the tops of the trees!

As the bus rolled along, Motor Mouse admired the views with his fellow passengers. They rode beside the canal. Then they crossed the river.

A fellow passenger offered Motor Mouse one of her Dairy Milk chocolate bars, and Motor Mouse felt so content that he nearly forgot all about his motorcar troubles.

At Shaftesbury Station, Motor Mouse gave the conductor
his ticket and hopped off to head for the flower shop.
He collected a large bunch of roses, then waited for Bus 15.

When it arrived, Motor Mouse climbed the stairs to the top. But when he stepped onto the upper deck, what should he find missing but . . .

THE ROOF!

This was a Green Line bus, and Green Line buses had open-air decks.

Oh dear, thought Motor Mouse. *The elements.*

He hoped it would not rain.

It rained.

Yet everyone on board remained quite cheerful. Many had brought along umbrellas just in case, and a very nice passenger shared his with Motor Mouse and the roses.

When Motor Mouse finally arrived at the Sleepy Hen Inn, the innkeeper was happy to see him. And she gave him a warm cup of tea in her parlor so he might dry out.

It is amazing what the lack of a car can bring, thought Motor Mouse as he sipped his tea.

At the end of the day, Motor Mouse walked over to Winston's garage, stopping to buy a dozen fresh scones on the way. How many drivers are lucky enough to have a mechanic as a friend?

At the garage Winston was delighted by the gift. No one had ever brought him scones before.

Motor Mouse told Winston about his double-decker day.
"Very nice, those upper decks," said Winston.
"Yes," said Motor Mouse.
Then he said goodbye and he started for home.

Oats delivery tomorrow, thought Motor Mouse as he walked.

He pulled a soggy timetable from his pocket.

Though he would miss his motorcar all week long, Motor Mouse knew that everything was going to be all right.

Double-deckers go everywhere! And they are full of kindness.

A Good Game
of Croquet

On nice summer evenings before dark, Motor Mouse enjoyed nothing more than a good game of garden croquet with his brother, Valentino.

They had been playing the game for years and they always played to win.

"Croquet is about winning," Valentino always said.

"Agreed." Motor Mouse always agreed.

The brothers were equally good, so each enjoyed his share of winning.

One day at twilight, Valentino was placing the hoops on the lawn for a game when he got a notion.

"I think we should play differently this time," he said to Motor Mouse.

"Differently?" asked Motor Mouse as he unpacked the mallets and balls.

"Yes," said Valentino. "I think we should play to lose. Loser takes all."

"*What?*" said Motor Mouse.

"Trying to win can make one so forceful," said Valentino.
"Force is good!" cried Motor Mouse.
"It does not contribute to world peace," said Valentino.

"Have you been watching that show again?" asked Motor Mouse.
"What show?" asked Valentino.
"That *Peaceful Planet* show," said Motor Mouse.

Valentino pointed at the sky.

"That cloud looks like your motorcar," he said to Motor Mouse.

"HAVE YOU?" asked Motor Mouse loudly.

"Yes," said Valentino, blushing.

"Whenever you watch that show, you want to save the world," said Motor Mouse.

"Yes," said Valentino.

"WELL, CUT IT OUT!" yelled Motor Mouse.

"You should use your peaceful voice," said Valentino.

"I DON'T WANT TO!" yelled Motor Mouse. "I WANT TO PLAY CROQUET, AND I WANT TO WIN!"

"Oh, all right," said Valentino. "It was just a notion." He picked up the red-and-yellow mallet.

Motor Mouse picked up the gray-and-blue mallet.

"Now, let's have a jolly good game," said Motor Mouse.

They tossed a coin. Valentino would go first.

Whack. Valentino's mallet knocked the red ball cleanly through the first hoop. He played on.

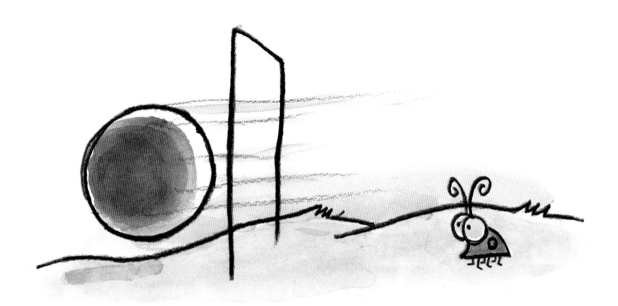

Whack. Through the second hoop.

Whack. The third.

Motor Mouse watched with his mouth wide open as Valentino's ball went straight through all the hoops until it hit the peg at the finish.

"How did you do that?" asked Motor Mouse.

"Peacefully," said Valentino.

"Oh, for Pete's sake," said Motor Mouse. "Well, I can match your score, and I will do it *forcefully*."

Motor Mouse positioned his blue ball.

"Prepare for astonishment," he told his brother.

Motor Mouse swung his mallet at the ball with all his might, and *whack*! He parked it right up against Hoop 2.

"What?!" said Motor Mouse. "I have never parked at Hoop 2!"

Valentino smiled.

"Maybe you should watch *Peaceful Planet*," he said.
"Oh, for Pete's sake," said Motor Mouse.

The game continued. But not for long. Because
Valentino ran his red ball through the hoops like butter
while Motor Mouse kept parking his blue one.

"You win," muttered Motor Mouse.

Valentino took a deep breath and slowly released it.

"I feel so peaceful," he said as he wrote down all his points on the scorepad.

"Well, *snap out of it*!" said Motor Mouse.

They prepared for a second game. But just as the game was about to start, a speeding bumblebee ran right into Valentino's nose.

"*Ow!*" yelled Valentino. "*Ow! Ow! Ow!*"

"Let me help you!" cried Motor Mouse. He quickly scooped some wet mud from under the roses and rushed to Valentino's aid.

Motor Mouse packed Valentino's poor nose in mud.

"Ow," Valentino whimpered.

"There, there," said Motor Mouse. "I will sing you a tune until the stinging stops."

Motor Mouse sang his tune. Valentino grew drowsy and went to sleep.

The croquet hoops and balls and mallets sat still as night fell.

When Valentino finally awoke, he felt much better.
"You are a nice brother," he said to Motor Mouse.
"Oh, stop it," said Motor Mouse. But he was pleased nonetheless that Valentino thought so.

"I don't know why I wanted to play to lose," said Valentino. "Winning is really fun."

"Yes," said Motor Mouse. "And next time, I intend to."

Then they packed up their croquet bag and walked to the house. Life was full.